Kalee Pinkpants

ISBN 978-1-64349-097-7 (paperback)
ISBN 978-1-64458-133-9 (hardcover)
ISBN 978-1-64349-098-4 (digital)

Christian Faith Publishing, Inc.
832 Park Avenue
Meadville, PA 16335
www.christianfaithpublishing.com

Printed in the United States of America

Kalee Pinkpants

In a House Full of Ants

JEREMY HENDERSON

alee Pinkpants was eating her lunch when two ants walked up and asked for a munch.

Kalee gave the ants some of her food without any doubt.

They were munching and crunching as they moved about.

Kalee went to the kitchen to get her a snack, and—

hey, what do you know—those two ants were back.

Except it just wasn't two ants anymore. Those two ants brought two friends, so now there were four.

Kalee gave the four ants some celery sticks.

Then two more ants showed up, so now there were six.

Kalee gave the six ants food and said, "This is the last time."

Then three more ants showed up, so now there were nine.

Kalee heard a small voice saying, "Hi, I'm Ben."

Ben is an ant, too, so now there were ten.

Kalee gave the ten ants food, her head blowing with steam,

and then seven more ants showed up, so now there were seventeen.

Kalee started yelling, "That's it! I've had enough! I'm sick of you ants that think you're so tough! I'm trying to be nice, and I don't mean to be rude, but I'm tired of you ants eating up my food."

Kalee heard a small voice saying, "I know what you mean." She turned around and there was the queen.

The queen told the little ants to get back home, and she wasn't going to say it twice, and she thanked dear Kalee for being so nice.

Kalee and the queen became really good friends as long as she never fed the little ants again.

The End!

About the Author

Hi! My name is Jeremy Henderson. I was born September 1, 1991, and I pretty much knew at the age of five that I was a walking ball of talent and charisma. I could sing, draw, dance, and I had the most insane imagination. I was always so fascinated with animals; at one point in my life, I wanted to be a veterinarian. But I was way too invested in creativity. I figured I rather draw animals all day than perform surgery on them. It took me a little time to figure out where I was going with my art, but like a true gift, it came to me one day with my vivid imagination and art skills that I can start a line of amazing children's books. I would like to add: don't ever give up on your dreams. We all have the power and ability to be anything we want to be. Thank you, guys, for reading.

CPSIA information can be obtained
at www.ICGtesting.com
Printed in the USA
LVHW021630040619
620070LV00007B/51/P

9 781643 490977